HOT & COCOA

SHENANIGANS

A SMALL TOWN HOLIDAY
SECOND CHANCE NOVELLA

DEBBIE
MITCHELL

HOT COCOA & SHENANIGANS

A small-town holiday second chance novella

BY DEBBIE MITCHELL

Published by:

ARCHER
Quill
PUBLISHING LLC

Cover Design & logo: Sweet Fifteen Designs
Editing by Book & Mark It Editing by Lexis
ISBN 13: 978-1-956988-25-3

Dedication:

*To my mom, who believes in me
And made me love Hallmark movies just
like her*

CHAPTER ONE

MADISON

Flying back to my hometown of Silverdale was not what I had planned. At least not until closer to Christmas. I was just about to sign the lease on my new apartment when I got the call. Mom said that my dad had an accident, and they needed me home immediately. Something about lights and a ladder was all I could get out of her. Me, being the over-thinker that I am, pictured him falling off the roof, laying in the snow and ice for hours. He probably sustained brain trauma before they found him. My mother told me he was laid-up in the hospital and his dying wish was to see his daughter before his end.

Well, of course, I got an Uber and rushed to the airport. I didn't even go home to pack. My dad is on his deathbed. Who has time to grab clean undies? At least that's what I thought. I rushed to the airport and desperately told the older woman at the ticket counter my situation. With her mouth open in shock, she tapped away at the screen. Luckily, there was one seat left on the next flight out. I made a mad dash to the terminal, waving my ticket in my hand right before they closed the gate. My thoughts run wild during the flight. I should have spent more time with him. When was the last time I told him I loved him?

When I rushed from the plane, I caught a driver waiting just outside the airport. I beg the guy to floor it to Silverdale Memorial. It's freezing here and me with nothing warm. He doesn't even make a complete stop before I'm tossing money to him and jumping out. Rushing into the hospital, frantically asking for Tom Hoover's room. I am hysterical by this point. My hands are resting on my knees as I catch my breath. The receptionist looks at me funny, but directs me to the Emergency Room.

There sits my dad in a bed as they are finishing up his cast. My parents are laughing at something the registered nurse says. My mouth drops open. This is not the man on his deathbed that my mother made it out to be.

"Laura, you win," dad nods his head towards the door where I'm standing.

Mom rises from her chair and wraps her arms around me. "You made it! In record time too!"

"Mom, you said he was on his deathbed!" I say a little too loudly. The male RN cocks his head at my mother.

"Now, that's cheating! No wonder you won the bet," dad says.

In confusion, I study my parents. "Bet?"

"Oh honey, I just broke my leg a wee bit. Your mother bet me you would drop everything and come to my side," he says, and gives her a glare. "I told her you would be here tomorrow. You wouldn't just drop everything for me. Didn't know she was gonna play the death card."

"So, are you okay? I mean, other than the leg," I ask.

"You're old man is right as rain," he says, sitting up straighter.

"Okay, Mr. Hoover, I officially discharged you. Make an appointment with your primary physician. Oh, and try not to do anymore acrobatics," says the doctor who just walked in.

My dad gives him a salute, then clumsily tries to rise off the bed with his new crutches.

"Where's your bags, honey? Let's get him home and settled," mom asks.

I give her the meanest look I can muster and growl between my teeth, "I didn't pack, MOTHER! You told me he was dying. I have no clothes other than what's on my back."

"I don't think I said he was dying, exactly," she says, and I tilt my head and stare. "Okay, so I might have made it sound worse than it was. How was I supposed to know it was only his leg? The ambulance wasn't even there yet."

I let out an enormous sigh. I guess I will give her a minor break. Apparently, like my father's leg.

She still could have let me have time to pack.

Thank God I still have clothes there from before

I left for college. Let's hope something still fits.

My kingdom for a sweater or coat right now.

We get dad loaded into the cab and I take my

place in the front, hovering over the heat vents.

"Where's your coat? Don't you know it's

wintertime?" the driver asks, and I turn and look

at my mom. She just smiles and shrugs.

Sometimes she can be so devious.

"So, what was the prize?" I ask.

"Hmm?" mom acts innocent.

"For the bet. What did you win?" I ask again.

"It really wasn't a bet, dear."

"Mom!"

"Okay, okay. If I won, he had to play Santa at

the fire department's Christmas party. Scrooge

here, didn't want to do it. You know how many

kids come to that party. Why, it's the entire

town," she says.

"Dad?" I ask.

"It's not important. I lost, so it doesn't matter,"

he says. That man is hiding something.

"So, you're not going to tell me?" I ask.

"I'd rather not."

"Tell me it's not something dirty," I plead.

"If it is, will I get out of telling you?" he asks impishly.

"Oh my God, yes! I don't want to know!" I say and cover my ears.

"Oh, for heaven's sake. If he had won, we would get Carl to be Santa, and he didn't have to introduce you to the new recruit at the firehouse. Tom, you are making it out to be a big deal. It's not like I'm asking you to make them fall in love, move back to Silverdale, get married, give me grandchildren. It was just an introduction. A little nudge, you might say."

"So, let me get this straight. I missed out on my new apartment, probably lost my job, all so I could be the pawn between Santa and a hook-up?" I ask, blown away. The driver chuckles and shakes his head.

"Oh Madison, I didn't mean for all that to happen," mom says, apologetically. Then, turns it around to suit her. "You really didn't like that job, anyway. Wouldn't you be happier in Silverdale? They don't appreciate you at that. What's it called? Bear Ruby's?" mom rattles off.

"Berube's. It's only the most well-known restaurant in Los Angeles. You have to work your way up, is all." I really didn't like it there. It would be years before I'd ever be promoted to head chef, if ever. Not to mention Alonzo would have to leave.

We pull to a stop in front of my childhood home. It's as beautiful and welcoming as I remember. The majority of the holiday decor is up. The tipped over ladder and a hanging strand of lights, evidence that at least the fall was true. Walking behind my dad like a parent ready to catch a toddler, I realize he is going to need some help. Mom can't do all that on her own. A little time back home wouldn't be so bad. It's only for a few weeks. I'll leave right after Christmas. It's a family emergency, right? If mom can convince me, maybe she can convince Alonzo. I have money saved. After all, it's been working and sleep for a year now. I haven't missed a day of work, and usually work doubles. There hasn't been a social life in I can't remember. I deserve this. Dang it! "Three weeks. I will stay until right after Christmas." Before she can jump with glee, I add to my mom, "and no matchmaking!"

"Cross my heart," mom says and makes the motions. Somehow, I don't believe her.

I decide, since I'm home, I'd cook supper. There are tons of recipes running through my mind. I make a list of what I need, scan the pantry, and borrow the car to head to the grocery store.

"Wow! You've sure mastered some cooking skills since you left. This is the fanciest thing I've eaten in years," my dad says, rubbing his belly. Mom gives him a poke. "You are a fantastic cook, Laura. When was the last time you cooked anything involving puff pastry, Gruyere cheese, and asparagus, though?"

"Fine. Yes, Madison has surpassed her mother in cooking. You'll never beat me at baking," she says and gives me a wink. I raise and lower my arms, bowing to the queen of all things desserts. She has me beat in that department. I hint at her she should remind me exactly how good she is

for breakfast.

CHAPTER TWO

MADISON

I awaken to the sun beaming in my window. You know the one. The snow and ice so thick outside that it makes the sunshine like a beacon. This comfy bed still calls to me, so I do what any other person would do. I roll over and cover my head.

I'm about off to dreamland again, when my mom comes in my room and plops down on the bed. "Madison, did I wake you?" I groan. "Can you help me with dad? He's having a horrible time with that cast and crutches. I'm making something special for breakfast." Mom sing-songs that last part. She makes the best breakfasts and knows I'm a sucker for that.

"Sure, mom. I'll be right behind you." Forcing myself to a sitting position, I roll my neck and stretch. I'm grateful that it wasn't worse, I think as I swing mine over and get up. As I pass the mirror, I take a glance. Oof. I forgot to take the scrunchie out before I fell asleep. My blonde hair I normally take pride in, now looks like I stuck my finger in a light socket. Not to mention, it's moved to the side of my head, a tangled mess.

"Sorry, Sleeping Beauty. I could have waited a little longer," dad says. He stifles a laugh when he sees my hair.

"All good, dad. We've got this." I throw my arm around him and help him stand. He does this clumsy, hop around thing until he can reach something to hold on to. Handing him the crutches, I encourage him to give them another shot. I'm not sure if he threw them last night, or he dropped them. There was no way he was going to be picking them up.

By the time we make it to the stairs, a waft of
fresh brewed coffee, bacon and something sweet
fills the air. Yes! Mom has baked her famous
Pumpkin Cinnamon French Toast Casserole.
With all the wonderful, mouth-watering smells
coming from the kitchen, dad and I practically
leap down the stairs. It was a sight to see. He's
trying to hop down as fast as he can. I'm rushing
too, but want to make sure he doesn't fall. Yeah,
we should have been more careful, but we are
talking made from scratch perfection here. Dad
and I stumble on the last step. He falls forward,
but catches himself. He learns those crutches
fast, because he's racing me to the kitchen and
puts one up in the doorway, blocking me from
coming in first. I put on my brakes and my
mouth drops open; him giving me a devilish
smile.

"What am I going to do with you two?" mom
asks. She shakes her head at us as she sets the
smaller baking pan on the table. She walks over
and pulls an even bigger one out of the oven.

"I'm starving, but I don't know if I can eat that much!" I say. Wondering what my mom is up to with the pan, big enough to feed a small army.

"Oh Madison, I was wondering if after breakfast you would drop this off at the fire station. With their captain gone, they won't know what to do with themselves," mom says.

I leer at my father. "While dad is an amazing captain, I'm pretty sure they can manage without him for a while." It's not like Silverdale is a vast town with fire alarms going off all the time. It's a charming, small town, where everyone knows everyone else. The last actual burning building they had was a year ago. They do a lot of fundraisers for the town, take on the small calls that come, and do practice drills to keep them ready for any big emergency. That's about as exciting as it gets, which is a glorious thing. They actually go door to door around the time change twice a year, spring and fall, and hand out batteries for everyone's smoke detectors.

"They are in the middle of planning the big Christmas party, the toy drive, the coat drive, the list goes on. The least we can do is bring them a casserole," mom says, one hand on her hip, the other waving a potholder around for emphasis. "And this has nothing to do with you fixing me up with the new guy?" I ask. Mom's mouth drops open, her hand on her heart. Being the dramatic southern belle, she is. Mom met dad when he came to South Carolina for spring break. After that week, he traveled home. They managed an entire month before they couldn't take being apart. Tom Hoover drove right back down to South Carolina and got his Laura. They've lived happily ever since. Oh, they tease and prank each other sometimes, and I've rarely seen a spat that got intense. They're made for each other, two sneaky peas in a pod.

I point my two fingers at my eyes and at their direction, indicating that I'm watching them. Grabbing a plate, I fill it with the morning spread. The delicious pumpkin casserole, more like a dessert, melts in my mouth. A satisfied groan escapes. She's made this before. But today, it's on another level. "You did something different?" both a statement and a question.

"I did. It's a secret." Mom leans in close, like she's going to tell me the secret ingredient, so I lean in to. She kisses me on the forehead and leans back, smiling mischievously. Like none of this took place, she eats. I slump all the way back in my chair, my arms hanging down. I can't believe she tricked me. About to ask what the secret is, mom continues talking. "Did you hear they closed down Cozy Corner?" My eyes grew enormous, and I almost choked on my bacon. Cozy Corner was THE place in Silverdale to eat and hang out. It's been around longer than me.

"Val & Stan?" I ask. Worry fills me. I know they were getting up there, but I'd hate to think about something happening to them.

"They're fine. Retired in Florida," dad assures me. I breathe a sigh of relief. He passes his keys across the table. "Might as well take the car when you go to the station. You might want to do something with," he looks at my hair and I feel my head. Oh yeah, the tangled mop up there.

I kiss him on the top of his head on my way
upstairs.

Searching through my closet, I realize my style
has changed a lot since I was living back home.
No wonder I left these things here when I
attended college. I come up with some plain
black leggings and some black work boots. The
boots left from my all-black phase. I pair it with
some bright and ugly Christmas sweater I had
gotten one year and refused to wear. Back in the
day, looking cool at all times was important.
Now, though gaudy, it makes me laugh and I'm
all about being happy. The nest that I call my
hair, needs tamed and applying a little tinted
Chapstick, eh, it will do. One more check on my
reflection, and I shrug. I pick up the keys dad
had handed me and jog down the steps, ready to
get this special delivery over with.

Mom hands me the big, covered pan and lays a
thermos on top sideways. In winter months,
mom always sent us with hot cocoa, just in case
we ever got stranded, we would have something
to warm us. Dad and I never got stranded. Well,

okay, once. It's how the warm thermos all started. We were out scouting for the perfect tree one year. I think I was around six. Dad hit a patch of ice and the car spun in a complete circle before stopping in a ditch. What did I say? "Let's do it again, daddy! That was fun!" No matter how hard he tried, the car wasn't moving. This was before cell phones were the norm. We survived on the warmth of the hot cocoa and stories until they rescued us. In reality, it was not even an hour. That's a long time for a kid. When we got home, I told mom how the only thing that kept us alive was the warm drink she had packed. Now, it's tradition.

The main street of town is full of decorations. The town is all tinseled up and ready for the holiday. It's really beautiful. I wave at a bundled family shuffling in the crosswalk to get to Meyer's department store. A little girl pointing at the doll in the window, yanking her father's arm to hurry. Santa standing in front of a shop, ringing a bell. Bellowing, a big, "HO HO HO," to those around. I smile, thinking about this town. Envisioned is its holiday beauty and how the entire town goes overboard for every holiday imaginable. I've been away from it for a while. When I get to the stoplight, I see the Cozy Corner ahead. I can't help myself and park in front of it. No brightly painted window of a Christmas scene. Just a For Sale sign. The building front drifts my mind back to all the good times I had there.

My first kiss was there. Transported back to another time, sitting at the corner booth with my first big crush. It was all sweet and innocent. We were sharing fries, and he was chattering away about the freshman football game. He was still in his uniform, covered in dirt and grass stains, but I didn't care. To me, he was the handsomest boy in school, and he liked me. The big doe-eyed stare I was giving him, my cheek resting on my hand. I laugh at the thought. Boy, did I have it bad for him. One of us dropped something, not remembering who anymore. We both bent down and bumped heads. When we raised them, our eyes locked. Neither of us moved for the longest time. So much so, it was getting awkward. To break the look, he quickly leaned in and put his lips on mine. I remember my eyes got really wide, then I closed them and kissed him back.

Awakened from memory lane by someone honking their horn. My eyes lift up to people waving, and I return it with a smile. Might as well get back on track and deliver the food. Putting it in reverse, I consider before backing into the street. The car behind me waves me out. Did I mention I miss this town? Yeah, everyone knows everyone else's business, but that kindness goes a long way in my book.

When I arrive at the station house, I grab the items, not even thinking about leaving the thermos in the car and head inside. The standard hello's, Madison's home, and how's Cap? going around. A vaguely familiar voice behind me startles me and I spin, the thermos flying. The man stretches out and catches it. His hand reaches out to hand it back to me. He is so incredibly handsome. He must be the "new" recruit. "*Not too shabby Mom*," I think. The man, however, seems familiar. Very familiar. His dimple deepens with his genuine smile. It's then I figure out where I know him from. My mouth tries to say the words as I take the thermos, but nothing comes out. I'm speechless.

CHAPTER THREE

HUNTER DEAN

"I see you still don't go anywhere in winter without the thermos," I say, chuckling. Remembering the story behind the thermos makes me smile. So many times, we shared the warm cocoa, sitting closely at Old Miller's Pond. Our cheeks and noses bright red from the cold, huddled together sharing the beverage. We skated there so often.

Madison looks even more breathtaking than I remember. Her blonde hair peeking out under her red winter hat. She looks more grown up. That's expected, I suppose, considering I moved away when I was fifteen. Five years can really change a person. The same eyes, yes. That body, though. My old flame has definitely grown up.

"Hunter? Is that really you?" she stammers out. I've surprised her, to say the least. The feeling is mutual. I never expected her show up at the station like this. She hasn't been home to visit her family since I moved back.

"Yeah, it's really me. It's been a long time," I say. *Why am I so awkward? It's been a long time. Really? That's what you going to say to her? Duh, Hunter, she knows how long it's been. You are the one who moved away.* My mind telling me exactly how *uncool* I've become. When I was the captain of the football team, I thought I had it all. In a way, I guess I did. I had her. Looking down, I scratch my head, trying to regain my composure.

When I look back up at her, our eyes lock. Flashbacks of our first kiss, her cheering for me at the games. My eyes instantly finding her in the bleachers, with no effort. That amazing smile she'd give me when I did. God, I've missed that!

So sweet, innocent, and it's still there. She's right in front of me. "Hey," I mumble.

She tucks a stray hair back behind her ear, pulling down her cap, before returning the "Hey." She looks down at the container of baked goods before pushing them forward. "Mom sent me over with these." I peel off the foil and take a whiff of the tasty treat.

"Here, let's set these down in the break room. How's your dad? I heard it's broken," I say, setting the food down on the table and grabbing two mugs from the cabinet. Clumsily, one falls, but I manage to catch it before it hits the floor. Madison had made a dive for it, too. She stopped when she realized I had it. "Oh, he'll be fine. The fact he's not here is probably hurting him worse than the leg. You know my dad," she says. Madison instinctively takes the mugs from me and is pouring the hot chocolate into the cups before sitting down. She pushes one towards me and nibbles at a little bite she's taken off the corner of the dish. She leans in the chair and pulls a foot into the seat, getting comfortable. I always loved that about her. "How's your folks? Are they back here, too?"

"Nah, they are now in Tahiti, sipping cocktails on a beach somewhere," I say. I stand, grab a couple of plates, and slide a slice to her. She shakes her head no. As we catch up though, she's taking little pieces with her fingers. Licking the crumbs off of them each time. Madison doesn't even notice she does it. Watching her talk, snack and lick the tips makes me chuckle softly.

"What?" she asks.

"Nothing. Just missed you," I say.

Her smile fades, and she gently pushes her chair back. "I've got to get going. It was good seeing you again, Hunter."

I hop up and stop her before she leaves. "Did I do something wrong?"

"No, not at all," she says, giving me a half-hearted smile that doesn't reach her eyes. It doesn't stop her from trying to leave.

"Maddie?" I call to her. She stops in the doorway but doesn't turn. "Are we okay?" I ask. Madison gives a slight wave without turning and rushes down the stairs. I'm fairly certain she was crying; I want to go after her. Just as I am about to, the siren goes off. The pull of wanting to chase her, overtaken by the need to serve. One more look out the window as she drives away, and I'm rushed by a team of firefighters trying to get past me to grab their gear. That's my cue. I hustle, throwing my gear on before jumping in the truck.

The Fire

I'm suited up, my SCBA on, self-contained breathing apparatus. I trudge along the interior, smoke and flames surround me. Scanning the home, finding the primary source, and hoping that I spot any movement. Part of the ceiling collapses to my left. I shield myself from any falling beams. Over the radio, I hear Cap ordering me to get out. Of course, that old man wouldn't miss this.

"I haven't found her yet. I've got this," I say into my mic.

"Hunter, get out of there now! That's an order!"
Cap calls out again.

Just then, I spot movement in the corner of the room. Mrs. Milligan is crouched down, her apron over her mouth, coughing and gasping for air. I lean down to her to help her stand, but she's already so weak. I take an oxygen mask and put it on her. She clutches it to keep it over her face. In one swift movement, I pick her up and start looking for the safest exit. There's no way we are going to go out the same way I entered. The moment I turn in that direction, the front of the house gives. I make it through the home, sometimes kicking through with my boots. We get to an exterior window. I set the elderly woman down momentarily, I bust out the window and grab the nearest rug to lie over the broken sill.

Thankfully, two of my team are just on the other side and reach for her as I pass her through the window. Quickly, she's out and taken further back. O'Malley's arm reaches in for me when a thunderous boom sounds from behind. I'm halfway out the window as more of the house collapsing in on itself. O'Malley yanks me tougher, and I do a tuck and roll as I leave behind the hopeless structure. The team has done everything they could to preserve it. It was just too late when we got the call. Luckily, someone driving by, phoned the fire station when they saw the smoke billowing from the old farmhouse.

Mrs. Milligan was safe and being taken in the ambulance to the hospital. She suffered smoke inhalation, and they need to establish she's okay. Reluctantly, I perch on the back of the second ambulance as they check my vitals and Cap chews my ear off for not listening to his authority. There's nothing I can do to get out of it, so I pretend to listen and just nod along. I know good and well he'd have done the same thing. He would have given his life to save that lovable old lady. Just like I was willing to do. My vitals are great, other than a rapid heartbeat, but that's to be expected. Apparently, he's finished when Cap puts his hand on my shoulder, nods at me, and hobbles away on his crutches.

I ride in the truck to the station in silence. The callback came from the ambulance crew that the elderly woman will be fine. My mind is fixed solely on one thing now. When can I be near her again? How do I win back the girl of my dreams?

CHAPTER FOUR

MADISON

Tears stung my eyes as I drove away from the fire station. That was the boy I was going to spend the rest of my life with. It broke me when he moved away. He swore we would figure out a way and make it work. At first, we did. Endless evenings on the phone until way past bedtime. Going to school looking like some sort of zombie from the lack of sleep and the mascara streaks that always seemed to be present. I missed him so much.

Weeks turned to months, and the calls got fewer and fewer, as he made a life in another state. He was a great guy, always the center of attention.

Of course, he had made new friends, and he got back into sports. The thought of him with another girl put me in a dark place. Everything about me was dark and cold. I wore black almost daily, like some sort of goth widow. Even my hair dyed to fit the ensemble. My parents were not happy at all about the change. I didn't care though; my heart was crushed into powder. At least, that's how I felt at the time.

I'm fairly certain that I took it a lot harder than he ever did. Flipping the visor down to look at myself, the mascara not nearly as ruined as the bargain bin brand of my youth. At least there's one plus. I dab at my eyes with a Kleenex I had found in the bottom of my purse; I make myself look presentable before I enter my childhood home. If I went in there all teary-eyed, I'd have to talk about it. There is no way I'm ready to talk about what I was feeling, even to myself. No, I would casually stroll into the house, giving off the vibe of not a care in the world.

I entered and saw mom, walking with a laundry basket on her hip. She gave me a weary smile.

Okay, something is up, and it has nothing to do with me. "Where's dad?"

"That man. I could wring his neck. He was watching TV and heard dispatch over that darn radio." She motioned to his portable CB radio that's linked to all the calls for the police, fire and ambulance. "Gertie Milligan's house was on fire. He made me help him into the truck and took off. That man has no business driving. I know it's his left leg that's broken, but darn that man! He wouldn't even let me drive him there. Apparently, I drive too slow for him." Mom let out a deep sigh. "Now, I'm worried about Gertie AND your father."

I take the basket from her arms and set it to the side before giving her an encouraging hug. "They are both going to be fine. You have to have faith." Taking the basket into the laundry room and filling the washer, it dawns on me. Hunter will be at that fire, and knowing that man, he'd probably be the first one inside. "Everyone is going to be fine," I tell myself softly and then take a deep breath.

Well, there is always one thing my mom and I have in common in a crisis. We head to the kitchen. While her forte is baking, the perfect measurements and exactness to it/ Mine is cooking with wild abandon. Who needs one level cup of sifted flour when you can put in a dash of this and a dab of that? I help her decorate the enormous lot of gingerbread men and Christmas shaped sugar cookies, in between the stirring and sauteing. By the time my dad makes it home, the house is scented with sweets and breads, mixed with garlic and tomato sauce. I use the oven sometimes; it's just reserved for yummy lasagna and buttery garlic bread.

When dad walks through the door and sees the sheer amount of food around the large kitchen, twice in one day... he knows he's in trouble. Yes, the first was probably the fact I'm home. The second gigantic feast is frustration cooking, and he knows it. As he passes me to take his punishment, he places a kiss on my cheek, "Hunter is fine."

By the time he reaches mom, my eyes are enormous and I'm trying to ask questions with a mouth full of sugary green tree with candy ornaments. "What do you mean, he's fine?" I ask, trying not to spit the cookie across the kitchen as I spoke.

"I, uhm," dad runs one hand through his thick salt-and-pepper hair, trying to also balance. "He's perfectly fine, dear. He ran in, got 'Ol Gertie out, easy-peasy." His hands motion like he is dusting them off. I quirk an eye at him. My hands on my hips as I tap my foot. "Okay, I'll be honest. I was a little nervous there for a while." My eyes grow larger before he continues. "He's fine, I swear! We checked Hunter out and everything."

"Dig your grave a little deeper, old man," my mom tells him, before shoving a cookie into his mouth to stop him.

"It's fine. I'm fine. It was a long time ago. What he does with his life is no matter to me." I say as I slam cabinets and grab foil and containers. Grumbling, I add cookies to containers, the icing getting all smeared as I pile them on top of each other before they are fully set. Under my breath, I growl, "If he wants to risk his life and throw all caution to the wind, that's his own business." SLAM, I set one of the heavy pans of lasagna on the counter and rip off a sheet of tinfoil. The piping hot cheese is going to stick to it.

"Madison, what on earth are you doing?" dad asks.

"I'm going to march right over there and see for myself! What do you think I'm doing?" I load up my arms and grab the keys off the counter. Mom rushes to the back door to open it for me. "And don't think I didn't see that smile between you two! We are not getting back together. I simply just need to see with my own eyes and all this food is going to go to waste. Might as well take it over there."

When I finally get everything loaded, and I'm buckling my seatbelt, my vision takes in the door. My parents are standing there, arms around each other, smiling and giving me a cutesy wave. I growl back at them. They actually laughed before turning back into the house. Oh, those two think they've won. I'll show them! I am not falling for those magnetic, earthy brown eyes with specs of amber that catch the light. Ugh. Let's face it, I'm still a goner when it comes to Hunter Dean. I must be strong. Three weeks. I can do this for three weeks. After twenty-one days, things become a habit, right? I've got this. As I pull up to the station, he's standing outside. Hunter turns to see me, and a beaming smile appears on his gorgeous chiseled face. I so don't have this. My head lies on the steering wheel. Get it together, Mad. You wanted to make sure he was okay, and you did that. I turn my head and peek up and out the window, not lifting my noggin from its spot. Yep, that very fine man is almost to the car, and I do not know how I thought this was a good idea.

CHAPTER FIVE

HUNTER

Well, it seems like I won't have to go search for the beautiful Madison. She's come to me. I stroll towards the vehicle when she sets her head on the steering wheel. So, this may not be as simple as I thought. I'll apologize for the past and drifting away from her after the move. Even grovel if I have to. Then, I convince her to go on a date. Ice staking at Miller's Pond and later dinner. I wish it could be at our booth where we used to go when we were kids, but unfortunately, that's not an option. Unless...

"Hey Madison," I say, as she finally climbs out of the vehicle.

"Hey." She draws out slowly. As she strides to the other side of the car and pulls the food out, she asks, "How's it going? Dad said you had a little trouble at the fire call."

I cringe. Why did he have to tell her about that? My fingers pass through my strands, and I take in a deep breath. "Yeah, I'm fine. Here, let me take that for you." She hands off part of the food she brought and fills her arms with the rest before using her hip to shut the door. We halted our conversation until we can get in and put it all in the kitchen onto the large table. When the rest of the crew sees us enter, they take the things she's carrying and follow us upstairs.

The assembly line has started as one person gets out the plates and sets them down, another doing silverware. Connie, the lead for the ambulance team, takes the cups down from the cabinet and fills the glasses. We share a building because of the size of the town. One side of the building holds the fire station, the other the ambulance service. In between, we share the kitchen, the "bunkhouse", a rec room, there are some offices, and two supply rooms. What we call the bunkhouse is a large room full of cots in rows, and lockers. I can't complain with the cots. They are better than your typical camping cots, with foam mattress pads on each one. Two-thirds of our team are full-time members and work a rotation, while the other third are volunteers. It's probably unheard of anywhere else but Silverdale. However, we wouldn't want it any other way. Our volunteers don't get called very often, but we keep them up on training exercises. Each one fills in two twenty-four-hour shifts a month to give the rest of the crew an extra day off, which is greatly appreciated.

Our big extended family gathers, and we all sit down to eat. Madison grew up with this crazy crew, since her dad's the captain. I'm positive she's heard all the stories a hundred times, but still laughs when they are told again. What can I say? They love her. What's not to love? Shoot, her bringing me here when we dated is the whole reason, I'm a firefighter.

We walk around the station after eating and end up in the rec room. "Foosball?" I ask as I spin a handle.

"Are we making bets?" she asks and smirks. We always made fun, little bets back in the day.

"Of course." Her hands make a gimme motion, waiting for what I get if I win. "If I win, we go on a date. Ice skating and dinner."

"Hunter..." she protests, but I stop her.

"One date, Madison. Come on, it won't kill you to go on one date."

"Fine. One date. Only if you win, though. If I win," she says, tapping her finger on her chin. "If I win, you have to dress up like an elf at the Christmas Party." I hold out my hand for her to shake and make it a deal. "Okay, Elfie, let's see what you've got." Madison is a lot better than I remember, and it's all I can do to win. There for a while, I was seriously unsure, and I couldn't have that. When I make that last winning shot, she throws her hands in the air and groans. She can get pretty competitive.

"Tomorrow, one o'clock, dress warm and bring the cocoa. Don't forget your skates." I say confidently. She seems nervous, but agrees. I walk her to her vehicle and open the door. There is nothing more I'd rather do than kiss her. I hold back, though. If I have to take this slowly, I will. My eye is on the prize.

The next afternoon, I drive up to her parent's home and pick her up. She gets into the passenger side, and I shut the door. As I walk around to my side, I look into the kitchen window and spot her parents smiling and giving me a thumbs up. Why can't winning her back be as easy as her parents? Tom and Laura Hoover are definitely on team Hunter for this one. We drive through town, and I turn up the radio. It's tuned to WCIL, all Christmas, all day. The two of us sing along to the music and even get some laughs when I bark along with the jingling dogs. The fact she looked longingly at the old Cozy Corner makes me smile. It is our "spot" after all. I pull up to Miller's Pond and shut off the engine, looking over to her. Madison's smile is so bright. I know this was a good idea. We find an empty bench and get our skates on. There are around twenty people there, and couples smile and wave as they skate by. One couple slides to a halt when they see us and the female excitedly says, "Maddie! You're home!" It's her friend, Sharon, and they hug and try to keep their balance as they catch up. Finally, the two just plop on the bench before they fall. The two girls are whispering and giggling, so Thomas and I decide to give them some time to catch up.

As soon as we are out of earshot, Thomas asks me if we are back together. I shrug, "I'm trying my best, man. I've only got a couple of weeks to win her over. Her dad says she's heading back the day after Christmas."

Thomas rubs his hands together. "Okay, so what's the plan?"

"I'm thinking, take her to all the places we used to go. Here, of course, and Cozy Corner for dinner." He looks at me, confused, until I pull the keys to the place out of my pocket and shake them.

"How did you manage that?"

"I may have told the realtor I was interested in buying it and wanted to check out the wiring and any fire hazards."

"You sneaky devil. Please tell me you're not cooking. I'm on call, and I don't want to leave Sharon and rush to the scene. I've got my own plans I need to work on."

"Hey! I'm not that bad of a cook." My friend gives me a look. He knows me too well. "I've got her parents in on it. There will be burgers, fries, and shakes all ready for us at five. The door is unlocked for them, and they promise to sneak out the back, sight unseen, when we get there. Hey, if you need some help with your project, I'll be there." We make one more trip around and join the ladies on the bench. I'm not sure what Sharon has been saying to her, but I think it's in my favor. The couple say their goodbyes, leaving us alone again.

Madison places her red gloved hand on mine and looks into my eyes. "Hunter, I know we have a long past. Just like you know, I have a life in

California." Maybe their talk wasn't as promising as I thought. "If you are okay with it, and you understand that no matter what, I'm leaving the twenty-sixth. We can spend that time together. I totally understand if that won't work for you."

I stop her from saying anything else. "Mads, I'll take it. Just make me a deal. No walls, okay? If something is bothering you, you tell me. Let's just live in the moment and not think about what happens after. Deal?" I ask.

She nods and pushes herself up from the bench. Holding her hand out to me, I take it and raise. We skate around the pond with ease, hand in hand. Occasionally, I maneuver us around and give her a spin and she returns with the most melodic, carefree laugh. Oh, how I've missed hearing that. On the last spin, I try to get fancy and we end up in a pile on the ice. My body leans over hers, my hands pinned under her. We are staring into each other's eyes, and I lean down to get that kiss. Right before our lips touch, a dog had run onto the pond and slid right into us. Tucker, Mr. Miller's dog, is slipping and sliding, tail wagging, giving Madison kisses on her cheek. I'm not sure if she's laughing at the doggie kisses or the fact, he got them before me. Either way, I sit up and rest my arms on my knees, sighing in defeat. That makes her laugh even more. She gets herself up and carries the big dog off of the pond. Ol' Tucker takes off for his next victim. Breathless and cold, we make our way back to the bench and I pour us some cocoa from the trusty thermos. My phone tings and I know that's the signal to get her to Cozy Corner. Time definitely flies when you're having fun. "Are you ready?" I ask.

"Oh, do you need to go? Was that a call?" she asks, with defeat in her voice.

"That was nothing. Just telling me it's time for our reservation," I say slyly.

"Reservation. In Silverdale?" she asks and chuckles. "Since when do we have a place that takes reservations?"

"You'll see," I say, and give her a wink. We put our other shoes on and walk to the truck, my hand on the small of her back. She tries to insist that she's not dressed for any place that would need reservations. "Mads, just go with it." She rolls her eyes but agrees to it.

CHAPTER SIX

MADISON

I thought for sure Sharon was going to murder me for not telling her I was back in town. I realize the fact I was there with Hunter was the only thing that saved me. She wanted all the dirt. I tried to convince her that there wasn't anything to confess. She wasn't having it. My best friend growing up gave me all the details about him moving back, how he hasn't purchased a home yet, but has been searching. She also filled me in on the fact there's been a couple of women in this town trying to catch him. Nevertheless, he only has eyes for me. He had obviously dated in high school and college, but they weren't

Madison Hoover, as she put it. Truth be told, I had the same problem dating. No matter how I tried, no one was Hunter Dean.

Still determined to make a life in California, I'd have to not get too caught up in my feels. Sharon told me I should tell him up front of my decision, but don't let it ruin the trip home. She said to have fun and let whatever happens happen. As long as I promised to make some time for her, too. I returned her the extremely binding pinky promise.

Hunter agreed to the time limit, and I agreed to let loose and live in the moment. I haven't acted this carefree in a long time. This is exactly what I needed. We skated and spun around the pond, reminiscent of how we used to. The two of us perfectly synchronized until we weren't. He tried to do some kind of Olympic turn and the next thing I knew; I was on the ground and his hands were around me. Bless this man, he made sure once he knew we were falling that I wouldn't get hurt. Of course, that meant we were pinned together. Looking up into those brown eyes, now at his lips, I bit mine. Would he hurry and kiss me already?

As it's about to happen and before I close my eyes, I notice Tucker running and slipping towards us really fast. There was no avoiding it. He was coming right for us. I did close my eyes, but it was for a completely different impact. Once Tucker got his bearings, he was attacking my cheek with slobbery kisses. Covering my mouth with my gloved hand, I had to avoid doggie tongue when I laughed. Trust me, I laughed. The dog, a mixture of who knows what, was a friend to everyone he met.

He's not mine, but Tucker would come over and visit a lot. I would perch on the porch swing, contemplating life. He would show up, jump up there with me, and lay his head in my lap. Contently, he would listen as I informed him why I was melancholy, joyful or clueless. I would caress his head as I continued on and on about Hunter, or after, which college to choose. He gave me one more big slurpy lick, and tried to trot around, skidding, and sliding. When

Hunter sat up frustrated that the tender moment passed, and that caused it to be even more humorous. My side was aching from it all.

Once the commotion died down, I carried the humongous pooch to the side. He barreled across the snow at his next victim, a little boy with a giant hotdog. Tucker wagged, his bottom shaking vigorously, wishing that the boy would give in. Apparently, the youth told him to sit and shake, because that's what happened. The youngster beamed and tore off a bite, tossing it up, the dog easily catching it.

Hunter's phone dinged, and he advised me we had reservations and had to get moving.

Reservations? In Silverdale? He escorted me to the truck, and we were on our way to eat. "Who on earth in Silverdale takes reservations, and why can't I change clothes for it?"

He says "Mads, just go with it." Of course, I rolled my eyes at him. Admittedly, my stomach gets a little fluttery when he calls me Mads. I stare at him when he's not looking. How did I not recognize him immediately? After all, we were a couple for a long time growing up. I think that was the reason. We both grew up. Oh, his eyes were and those dimples a dead giveaway, once I got a good look. However, his face had changed, gotten fuller as a man does, more masculine. Don't get me wrong, I loved this grown Hunter. He was even dreamier than when we were young.

The truck stopped before I realized, and we are parked. When I looked out the front window, I gasped. We were at Cozy Corner. I gave him a confused stare, since I know it's shut down. He gave me a cocky smile and led me inside. My hands quickly covered my open mouth when I saw it, our booth. It was all set up with our favorite meal there. Burgers and fries with chocolate shakes. Except today, there was a lit candle on the table, too. My hand grazed over the jukebox, feeling the rounded curves. Touching the screen, I reminisce about the songs and moments of this place. So many memories. Not only with Hunter, but with friends. Sharon and I close together, giggling about boys, pretending to be picking out a song. Truthfully, it was more like filling each other in on anything the other had missed. Who was smiling at who, and which girl got asked to the dance. Of course, I couldn't forget the "Is he looking at me? What's he doing?" questions one or both of us would ask the other. I place my palm flat on the machine and smile. Before I step away and turn back to Hunter, I push A-14 with my fingertip and an all too familiar song plays. I had to ask, "You did all this for me?" I turn around, taking in the rest of the place. "But how?"

He smiles at me and helps me out of my coat. "I have my ways," is all he said. Hunter pulls the cap off my head and I quickly try to brush down my hair with my fingers while he's turned away, hanging our coats on a rack by the door. As he strolls back over, he holds out his hand. I take it and he pulls me in close for a slow dance. Much closer than back in school, where we had to keep space between us. No, this was more intimate, with my head on his shoulder. His arm wrapped around me; I feel the heat of his body against mine. When the song is over, he places his hand on the small of my back and leads me to the booth. I've always loved the gesture. There is just something about having a masculine hand there, gently leading you on. It's just, I don't know, sexy.

CHAPTER SEVEN

HUNTER

The surprise on her face made it all worth it.
Even missing out on the kiss. Darn dog. She
never expected this is where I was taking her.
She was staring at me the whole way here. I
pretended like I didn't notice. Madison, staring
at me dreamily, benefits me. I need all the help I
can get if I'm going to make her fall back in love
with me in the little time I've got.

"You did all this for me?" she asks. "But how?"
she turns in a circle, looking around.

"I have my ways," I say, and give her a wink.
Surely, she remembers, possibly she doesn't, but
that's our song she's playing. I can't hold back

any longer and pull her into my arms for a dance. Her head lies on my shoulder, and I take in the scent of her shampoo. Nuzzling into her neck, I get the softness of her perfume. Something floral and feminine. As I finally get up the nerve to kiss her again, the song ends and we part. Will I ever get the chance to kiss her? This would be comical if it was happening to someone else. A deep sigh leaves me, and I decide to roll with whatever karma deals me. I swear I've been a good guy. I save people and everything. With my hand on the small of her back, I walk her over to our favorite spot, all ready for us. "Your seat, madam." Madison slides over and makes room for me. Exactly like the good old days, side by side, we sit.

She takes a French fry and dips it into her shake before taking a bite. "Yep, it's how I remember it," she says with a smile. Without a beat, she waves her fry at me. "You got my parents in on this, didn't you?"

"Me? Your parents? That's crazy. I mean..." I try to play it off, but I'm a horrible liar. "Here." I say and try the whole dipping a fry thing and holding it out to her. I never understood the whole appeal. Fries belong in ketchup, not ice cream. "It's just how you remember it, Mad."

"Oh, it's exactly how I remember it, all right. How I remember it from my own house! This is not Cozy Corner fries. This is Laura Hoover fries!"

"Nah, couldn't be," I say, trying to act surprised. Taking a few, dipping them in the red condiment as God had intended, and shoving a mouthful in. If I keep my mouth full, I can't get into trouble. "Hunter Dean! If you don't fess up, I'm outta here," she proclaims and scoots. I grab her arm and try to choke down the fries quickly so I can speak. Wrong move. My eyes grow large. A fry is stuck. She jerks her arm back and looks at my face and panics. "Hunter! Are you okay?" She's slaps me on my back and raises one of my arms. I shake my head. How do I tell her I need a drink when I can't say it? The shake is way too thick. I try to mime a glass of water. "Water? You need a drink?" I nod and she scoots around and dashes off to the kitchen. In the meantime, I'm trying hard to swallow it down and hit my chest with my fist. Like that's really gonna help. Quickly, she's at my side, handing me a glass of water, and I quickly chug it. It's painful, but I get it to wash down. I gulp in air. "Are you okay?" she asks again.

This time, I can answer. "Yeah. That was kinda scary. See what you did?"

"What I did?" she exclaims. She is about to tear into me when she sees a grin on my face. "Ugh! You, Hunter Dean, are a horrible man." At least, it gets her to plop by down and scoot over. Madison grabs the fries and pulls them over to her, out of my reach. "You, mister, lost fry privileges."

"Fair enough," I say, before I take a small bite of my burger. Nothing else can happen. We sit in silence, eating for a few minutes. Finally, I speak up. "So, maybe, just maybe, I had a little help from your folks. Is that so bad?"

She sighs before answering. "Yes, they like you, Hunter. They like us," she says, motioning between the two of us. "I don't think I'm ready to go back there. When you left, it broke me-bad. Really bad. I get you had no control over moving. That's not your fault. But it doesn't mean it still didn't kill me."

I place my hand on top of hers. "We both hurt. If there was any way I could have stayed, believe me, I would have. You were my girl, I love you."

"Loved," she corrects. "You loved me."

"No, I'm pretty sure I said it right," I tell her softly, then pull her hand to my lips and kiss it. She smiles back, but it's not real. I lower her hand and she drags it back and places it in her lap. Sitting back further in the seat, I look at her. My head lifts towards the ceiling. My face in my hands. I groan before looking back at her. "But you don't feel the same. Do you?"

"I don't know what I feel. You came back to Silverdale. I left, and you came back. Everything here reminded me of you, and it hurt. You've obviously been making plans and talking to my parents. This. This has all been kind of sprung on me, ya know? I need some time to process this."

I give her a nod of understanding. My chest is tight, and my heart is shattered, but I understand. There's no other choice.

The ride to take her home was quiet. All but the soft sounds of the radio playing Christmas tunes. Madison's head is propped on her closed hand as she stares out the passenger window. Her other hand lies on the seat. I want to hold it, take it in mine. Fear of making it worse stops me. What do I do or say to make her understand that I'm here to stay now? She won't have to worry about getting hurt again. I'm here. I'm right here.

When I pull up and park the car in her parents' driveway, I look over at her, unsure of what to say. She turns to me and gives me a soft smile.

"Thank you for today. I know it's not how you planned it ending. It was thoughtful and sweet though, and I want to thank you," she says. Madison takes my hand in hers. "Just so you know, I have feelings for you. I probably always will. There're just things I need to sort out in my head, okay?"

"Okay," my only reply.

"I, uhm, promised Sharon I'd spend some girl time with her while I was home. Just give me a day or two to sort things out. I've got a life in California. A job... well, I think I still have one."

"Can I ask for one thing?"

Hesitantly, she answers, "Sure."

"I have tried and tried. Can I please just have a goodnight kiss?" I plead.

Madison laughs, obviously reminded of the Tucker incident from earlier. She nods and leans in closer. My fingers slide around her neck, intertwined in her hair as I pull her forward. Our mouths slightly part and our eyes slowly close as I press my lips to hers. Madison's pillow-soft lips are even better than what I remember. Our kiss deepens, and she rakes her fingers through my short, dark hair. As we take a breath, our foreheads pressed together, I feel a smile emerge on her lips as they barely touch mine. It makes me smile too. She whispers, "I better go," giving me one last quick peck and letting herself out of the truck. I watch her until she unlocks the door and gives a small wave before it closes.

CHAPTER EIGHT

MADISON

With my back pressed against the door, I sigh and touch my lips. And that folks, is why I have compared every single kiss to him. A small giggle escapes me, and I rush upstairs to my room. In the window seat, I watch as his taillights travel down the snow-covered road until they disappear. So maybe it wasn't such a bad date after all. I shoot a quick text to Sharon and ask her about shopping tomorrow. I need some clothes that aren't circa high school. She's all in. Tomorrow is girls' day, and I can't wait to hang out with my friend.

Dad hasn't needed my help as much as I thought. He has mastered the crutches and is hopping around the house faster than me. That wonderful man even had the coffee brewed when I came downstairs. "You are my favorite person right now," I tell him as I pull a mug out of the cabinet and kiss his cheek.

"Don't let your mom hear that," he replies.

"You're up early. What are your plans today?" He asks and passes me the creamer. I pour the creamy liquid into my cup and stir. Ah, the aroma of coffee and vanilla fills my nostrils.

"Sharon and I are going to go shopping and hang out," I say, my back up against the counter, taking my first long sip. Heaven in a cup.

Moments later, there's a knock at the back door. I let Sharon in. She's all smiles as she gives me a hug and another for dad. Dad hands her a cup and pours the coffee, staying balanced. He really has bounced back quickly.

"Thanks, Mr. Hoover. You're my hero."

"You guys keep this up and I'm going to give up fire chief and become a barista," he says and adds, "Is it the same if it's male or female? What's a male barista called?" Sharon and I look at each other and shrug.

"He's called a pain in my..." moms says as she enters the room. "Good morning, girls. Sorry about breakfast. I can't believe I overslept."

"You know you don't have to cook for me every morning. Relax. Do what you normally do when I'm not here," I say.

"So, she should cook up schemes to get you to come home?" dad said under his breath.

"Tom! I heard that!" mom says. I'm hiding my smile behind my big cup, trying my best not to laugh. She walks over to me, grabs my head, tilts it and kisses me. "Well, it worked, didn't it? My girl is home." I love my parents. Yeah, sometimes they can be over the top. It's all done in love, though.

The day is warmer than it has been. The streets and roads have been cleared. What once was compacted white, is now little more than slush. I smile, trying to imagine an L.A. native trying to drive up here. While the traffic there sometimes makes me cringe, the sheer amount of snow and ice we have here would cause that city to shut down.

Sharon and I are talking a mile a minute. It's like no time has gone by at all. I love friends like that. You can both go do your thing and when you get to see them, it's back to where you were. She fills me in on her and Thomas. I fill her in on what few guys I've dated over the years. While telling her about one particularly awful date, she wrinkled her nose as if something had died. I couldn't help but laugh. We spent the morning finding the perfect pair of jeans. Passing on the ones I had to jump several times and suck in breath to get into. "Remind me to slow down on all the comfort food. I need a salad for lunch," I tell my friend.

"Why on earth would I do that? It's finally giving you a booty," she says with a laugh. I turn to check the mirrors and my behind. I have to say, this last pair of jeans makes me have actual curves. So, what does a smart girl do? I buy a pair of all three shades. After that, we check out another shop for some Christmas gifts. Found the perfect gift for mom and also picked up a couple of toys for the Christmas party. We run into a couple of friends and decide to do lunch.

Across the street, is the Cozy Corner. I gaze longingly at the for-sale sign. Man, I wish I could come up with the money to buy it. Is that what I really want to do, move back here, and become a business owner? "Hey, earth to Madison. Are you gonna throw those in the trunk?"

"Oh. Yeah, sure," I say and put them in there and close the lid.

"So, you thinking about high school or last night?" my friend asks about my distraction and the building.

"Truthfully, neither. I was kind of thinking about buying it," I reply.

"Really? That would be so cool! So, you're thinking about moving back?" one of the girls asks.

I shrug. "I don't know. Just daydreaming, I guess." My friend loops her arm into mine and we walk down the sidewalk towards the restaurant further down the street. It's a couple of blocks away and the only place left to eat in this area. Any other place is on the other side of town. Granted, we're not talking a thirty-minute drive or something. But there could be more options here, without hurting the other's business. Like a "nice" place to eat on a date. We really don't have that here in Silverdale. Couples usually go out of town on special occasions. The wheels in my mind turn.

Trying to stay in the moment and into the conversation with the three other ladies at the table has become difficult, to say the least. It's not that they aren't interesting. They are. It's just that I can't seem to stop coming up with design plans and menus for that place. This would take a lot of work to get it from high school hangout to an elegant eatery. It can be done, though. The next thing I know, we're standing and hugging our goodbyes to the other two. I look down at my plate and yes; I ate. It's crazy, but I don't even remember it. "I am so sorry, you guys. My mind was just... I apologize."

"It's all good, really. You've had a lot going on since you've been back. What with your dad's accident and seeing Hunter after all this time. We get it," one girl says and the other nods.

"Yeah, it's just been a lot," I say. That's not really it at all, but how can I tell them I'm fantasizing about a restaurant instead of keeping up with the conversation. Sharon gives me a wink and rolls with it. Only my best friend could possibly know how my mind wanders, and there's no stopping the freight train once it gets rolling at full speed.

After the other two leave, she pulls me back to the table. "Okay, give me all those brilliant ideas you've been dreaming up for the last hour." And that's what I do over dessert, fill her in on all the ideas and plans for the place. She's just as excited as I am, and that's why I love her. Getting all these thoughts out somehow releases them, and now I can focus on reality. Which happens to be finding some cute tops and an outfit for the party.

We stroll over to a boutique and find the perfect dress. Then a department store for some shoes and a gift for dad. Once the search is over and the items are in the cart, I notice the lingerie department and push the cart in that direction. "I need to pick up a new bra, some pajamas and some undies. If I'm going to be here for a couple more weeks with no luggage, I need to stock up."

"Ew, please don't tell me you've been wearing the same underwear since you got home," she says.

"Seriously?" I say and give her a hip check. "I had clothes at home that I had left. They are just things I don't normally wear. Case in point," I say, and point at the outfit I'm currently wearing. A pair of black jeggings and an over-sized hoodie, finished with chucks and very colorful socks.

"I see your point," she says and takes the cart from me and makes a B-Line to the department.

The next ten minutes are us holding up undergarments and either approving or nixing them. When she holds up a sexy pair of panties and insists that I may need them, raising and lowering her eyebrows mischievously. I out-do her, and hold up something even more risqué and wave them in front of me. The next thing I know, a little old man walks by and stops, giving me a thumbs up. I am going to curl up and die right here. Sharon is trying to control herself until the man walks off and it's all she can do not to bust out laughing.

Then, it gets worse. I look to see someone that has stopped to see what the old man is giving the thumbs up for, and it's him, Hunter freaking Dean. I bury my face in my hands, which unfortunately still holds the panties. My bestie looks over that direction, spies Hunter, and that's it. She busts out laughing so hard that everyone in the area within earshot is looking. I peek up through the lace and see a huge smile on his face. He then also gives me a thumbs up. I throw the panties in the cart and my head towards the ceiling and groan. It's then I make my way to the checkout as quickly as possible, looking straight ahead. My friend following behind me, still cackling.

CHAPTER NINE

HUNTER

Seeing her holding up sexy panties today made my day. Of course, I'd love to see them on her. It wasn't just that, though. It was her, hanging out with her friend and having a good time. Madison being her carefree self. No worrying about how she feels or how I feel. Just her cutting loose and not brooding over anything. That, right there, is the girl I fell for.

I leave the store with a spring in my step and a renewed outlook on everything. It's all going to work out. Faith in the future from just a small, simple act. Insignificant to some, but at this very moment I know. Everything I've hoped and dreamed of is going to come true. I hop in the truck with the tool my friend Thomas needed, and head over to his house. Thomas and Sharon are married, and have been for a couple of years now. The girls are out doing their thing and I'm here to help him build the surprise library/office that Sharon has always dreamed of. That's her Christmas gift. She's always wanted a cute little office area with a book nook, and he wants to give it to her. I think it's sweet and if I can help him make that happen, I will.

It's upstairs in the attic and she has absolutely no clue. He works on it every chance he gets while she's gone to work or out. He has checked on her a few times today already, sending texts here and there to find out what time he has to hide the tools and supplies. She never goes up there, so that's not a problem. He just doesn't want to leave any clues lying around.

"I just spotted them at the department store. I'm not sure if they were going anywhere else, but at the very least, she has to take Madison home. Do you want me to text Mrs. Hoover, and get her to stall if they show up?" I ask.

"Yeah, thanks. We need a couple more hours if we're going to get it ready by Christmas. There is still the shelving to finish. The floors and walls are done. If we can get those shelves knocked out today, we can start getting the rug, desk and decor done. The books will be last. That woman would notice if any of her books go missing."

"I'm on it. Mrs. Hoover is going to sucker them into decorating. Since Cap can't climb or anything, she needs the help," I say. "She'll text me the second she leaves."

"Bless that woman. You know, you're pretty lucky to have them in your corner," he says, while screwing in the pieces for the shelving. I nod in agreement while holding the other end in place. We work diligently to get everything done as quickly as possible. Stopping for a beer and admiring our work once all the bookcases were in place.

"Not too shabby for a fireman and cop," I say and take a swig from the bottle. I feel the phone vibrate from my back pocket and pull out my phone. "She's pulling out of the driveway now. Better get the rest of the stuff up here quick." We set down our beers and rush downstairs to grab the rug, and other items that were delivered while we were working. We dash downstairs and plop on the couch and turn on the game just as she comes through the door, none the wiser.

"Hey there, Hunter. Hi, babe," Sharon says, and walks over to kiss her husband. "Madison's mom sent me home with food. There's plenty if you're hungry, Hunter."

"I'm starved, thanks. So, how did shopping go?" I ask with a laugh.

"Wouldn't you like to know? Guess you're going to have to find out," she says slyly. "Babe, would you mind grabbing the rest of the bags out of the car for me?"

"Sure, hon. Be back in a sec," he tells us.

Once the door shuts, she leans across the table. "She wants to buy Cozy Corner. It's all she could think about. Well, not all she could think about, but that was the major thing. If she can figure out the how, we can get her back home for good. Can you think of anything?"

"Are you serious? She's considering moving back? Don't play with me, woman. I need this!" I say, leaning across the table. When he comes back in with the bags, he sees us huddled together, conspiring.

"Is there something I need to know?" Thomas jokingly asks, knowing that there is no way I'd go after his girl.

"Nothing, dear," she replies, trying to sound innocent. That's when panic reaches his eyes, and he drops the bags.

"You didn't tell her, did you?" he asks with fear. She crosses her arms and looks at her husband, "Tell me what?" Now, she's looking at me for answers. How do I get myself into these things?

"I swear, dude. We were talking about Madison," I say, throwing my hands up in front of me.

"Okay, spill it. What's going on?" she asks with determination.

"He thought I might have told you what he got you for Christmas." My friend's eyes grow huge and full of anger until I continue. "He got you something and had me hide it at the station. He was afraid you weaseled it out of me." Relief washes over his face.

She squeals, "Oh, you sneaky man. What is it? No, don't tell me. I want to be surprised. Is it big? Is it small, like a jewelry box? Seriously, don't tell me." She jumps up from the table and wraps her arms around her husband and gives him a big kiss. "Okay, I'm going to go take a bubble bath. Between the all-day shopping and then all the decorating, I deserve it. You two eat and plan how we are going to keep our girl in town. You, mister. I'll see you upstairs after shortly." She gives him a wink and another kiss and practically skips upstairs. We both give an enormous sigh of relief, before I give him a little punch in the shoulder and a laugh. He is, after all, a lucky man. I wolf down the food and let myself out. After all, he's got a beautiful wife upstairs and a night full of fun ahead.

Me, I've got a station to get to and hopefully a night to relax and come up with a way to make Madison's dreams come true. She's going to get that restaurant, if I have to use all my money for a home to do it. It's going to happen. Of course, if I use all my savings for the restaurant, where would we live? Yeah, maybe I'm presumptuous, but we will be married and needing a home. Isn't that how dreams come true, though? Believing in them.

Once I'm back at the station, I'm sitting with a notebook on my bed. Lists are made and ideas to make this happen are formed. Some are pretty hair-brained, some have potential. I scratch out those that have no chance, ripping them out, wadding them up and tossing them into the trash. When I have a decent list of ideas that might work, I lay back in bed, one arm bent and under my head, studying the list. Satisfied, I lay the notebook down and drift off to sleep.

Thankfully, the next morning is free of alarms, and I make calls to see what I can do. Things are finally looking up. "Oh, this is going to happen,"

I tell myself and grin. Everything is falling into place. Another shift at the station, gathering up the items donated around town for the coat drive and toy drive, and getting everything gathered for the party. Tomorrow I will go over to the Hoover's house and win her heart, again.

CHAPTER TEN

MADISON

Mom, dad, and I finished up the decorations yesterday. Today is going to be making more Christmas cookies and goodies for all our friends and neighbors. Then tonight, we go caroling, giving the people of Silverdale, song and sweets. It's Hoover family tradition. If you thought mom's baking was in overdrive when she was worrying about dad, you have seen nothing yet. This is what Laura Hoover lives for.

After we feast on yet another big breakfast, we get the kitchen cleaned up and start gathering all the ingredients of flour, sugar and all the secrets of cookie and candy making at its finest. From fudge to divinity, gingerbread to Christmas crack, every sheet pan and cooling rack is covered. This mother-daughter team is unstoppable. That is, until there is a knock at the door. Dad maneuvers around us to answer and who walks through the doors, Hunter Dean. "Hey, Mrs. Hoover, Cap. Hey, Mads," he says. We all say hi back and I stare at my mom in question. Dad pulls him through the room and tells us he had Hunter to come over to fill him in on how the coat drive and toy drive went. Okay, that makes sense. No ulterior motives by the parents. That's a relief, and kind of shock. Mom and I continue in our assembly line of treats. I fill containers to make room for the other things that need to go in and out of the oven. Every once in a while, I peek into the living room to check on the guys. They are deep in discussion each time.

Mom loads more of the baked goods into the oven and begins making another batch of sugar cookies, when she announces, "I'm out of almond paste and the pretzels are missing for the white chocolate."

My father walks in carrying an almost empty bag. "You mean these pretzels?"

"Tom! Well, you're just going to take me to the store and help," mom tells him. "I'm making a list."

"Mom, I'm sure there is enough here to put half the town in a diabetic coma," I say.

"Well, then that's it. I need a lot more," she says.

I put my hand on my hip and raise an eyebrow.

"You said half the town. I'm not leaving the other half to suffer. Tom, grab your coat. Don't forget the stuff in the oven, Madison. Oh, and can you get started on the fruitcakes? I'm sure Hunter would love to help. Don't you, Hunter?"

"I don't know if I'd be much help with that. I would be happy to run to the store for you," he answers.

"Don't be silly. I'll go. It will be so much faster. You two have fun," mom says. Swiftly makes a beeline out the door, while pulling my dad behind her, they leave.

Hunter stands in the middle of the kitchen, scratching his long, calloused fingers in his short hair. Bless his poor, confused heart. I motion for him to come over to the other side of the counter and slowly he does. I placed the biggest bowl I can find in front of him with a grin from me. Then, the flour, eggs, sugar, and recipe. "Here ya go," I say. I toss him a ring of measuring cups and he almost misses. "That was close, quarterback. You almost fumbled. Does anyone really eat fruitcake?"

"I happen to love fruitcake," he announces. Then he dusts his fingers with flour and flicks it into my face. I flinch and jump back in shock. "And I... do not... fumble." Another flick.

Oh, it's on! Reaching and grabbing the container, I grab a generous handful and over-hand throw it. The white cloud sifts between the two of us. The majority, covering his hair and face. He comes towards me, but I tuck the container under my arm like a football, twisting and faking a turn. I dash around a chair and put it some distance between us. Hunter reaches over the

chair and grabs my free arm. He pulls me
towards him and the chair tips. Then the
scoundrel shakes his head at me, flour flying off
of him and onto me. While I'm distracted, he
grabbed a huge handful and dumps it onto my
head. I get free and push my body backwards.
Lowering the container to my knees in front of
me, I swing the whole thing in an upward
motion. All the kitchen now dusted white.

Not to be outdone, Hunter grabs the nearest thing
and starts throwing it, sugar. We both stare
across the counter at the egg carton, then at each
other. Each diving for it at the same time. As I
pull it away, I grab a couple. Hunter, realizing
he's about to be scrambled, holds his arms out in
front of him and slowly backs away as I inch
forward with a devious smile. "You don't really
want to do this," he pleads.

Step by step, I make my way towards him. "Oh,
yeah. I believe I do." It's then his back hits the
counter. The realization that he's now trapped
shows in his wide eyes. Rapidly shaking his head
no, flour still falls from his head. "You're

trapped. Time to face your punishment," I say. One egg smashed against his chest, the other onto his head. He's dripping with goo as I rub it into his hair. "It's fantastic for you. Your hair is going to shine."

"Uh huh," he answers. "Better get this cleaned up." What I didn't realize though, he reached behind him and grabbed the sprayer and proceeds to hose me down with water. I'm trying to reach around him and shut it off. He's got his other arm wrapped around me, holding me close. The exchange, the water, the egg, we both start slipping and the next thing, we are on the floor of the kitchen. We gaze at each other, seeing that the other is fine, and burst out laughing hysterically. He rakes some of the runny yolk mixture off of himself and slides it down my hair.

We end up wrestling around on the floor. On the last big roll and flip motion with my leg and arms, we hit the island and look up. Just in time to see a bowl of cherries tumbling off the counter for us. He grabs me and rolls us to safety as it hits the floor. "Aww, you saved me," I say, pinned under him.

"Nobody likes fruitcake anyway," is his reply. I gasp, and he takes me into a kiss. The same butterflies I used to feel so many years ago are fluttering around in my stomach again, and I kiss him back. Our bodies completely covered with enough batter now to make a cake; we sink into the moment. A moment, cut too short when a key turns in the lock. We didn't have enough time to jump up, however, we sat up and separate a few inches. His pinky entwines with mine as we face the firing squad.

"What the..." it's my dad's voice above the squeak of the door opening wide. I suck in a breath and hold it, but neither of us move. The footsteps round the island we are behind. The grit of the sugar, like sand on pavement, as they walk. Sheepishly, we watch the two standing above us. At the same moment, we point to the other and call out, "They started it!" Mom glares down at us, but dad tries to hide the upturn of his lip. At least one of them won't kill us. I use

Hunter's shoulder to lift myself up to a stand. Once I'm up, I hold out a hand to help my accomplice to his feet. My foot slips, and he catches me. The rolling of my mother's eyes before she turns and heads towards the oven. Apparently, we hadn't noticed the smell of something burning. She takes the two burned cookie sheets out of the oven, walks around us, dumping both into the sink. They weren't the only things steaming.

"Mom, we will clean this up. I swear!" I hate seeing her mad.

"Oh, I know you will. Both of you." She gives us each a look. Hunter nods, keeping his eyes lowered. She pushes a broom into his hand. Me, I get the sting of a wet towel spun up and flicked at my leg.

"Ow! That hurt," I say. Mom tosses me the towel and motions to the mess with just her head. My cue to get to cleaning. She grabs my dad at the elbow and carefully steps over any mess she can as he leads her back out.

I hear my dad whisper, "I told you nobody likes fruitcake." Hunter looks at me, and I at him. The second they are clear from hearing, we burst out laughing again. We spent the rest of the day cleaning up our mess. It was far more fun making it, than cleaning. I still say it was worth every grueling hour.

CHAPTER ELEVEN

HUNTER

Cleaning the kitchen was absolute torture. At least it was fun while it lasted. When I finally got the last bit clean, I asked her if she forgives me for leaving. She plopped down in the wooden chair, exhausted, and turns her head to me, "Yeah, I do. Do you still have the energy to walk around town delivering cookies and caroling?" She eyed me closely. I knew she was as tired as I was, but if she's going, I will follow. I dramatically throw my head back and roll my eyes, pretending to be dreading this. She throws the dish towel in her hand at me, and I catch it in midair and smile. "Drama king. So, meet you at the firehouse in an hour and a half?" I rise out of the chair and kiss her forehead. Reaching into my pocket, I pull out the keyring and leave out the back door. "Was that a yes?" I call out. "I'll be there, ready to go." The drive was quick, and I stood under the hot, steamy shower of water, trailing down my body. I close my eyes and let the beads fall across my face. Madison and I had a good day, a great day. Thinking of her, covered in goo, and rolling over to kiss her. One day, I will kiss that woman and nothing and no one is going to interrupt us. Heat pelting down on my aching muscles relieves me, invigorates me. It's exactly what I needed. I'm not much of a singer, but I'm ready to belt out some tunes. Bring it on, Hoover family. Let's carol.

I hop down the stairs, two at a time, ready to greet the trio. My feet screech to a halt at the bottom of the steps when I see them. They are dressed up. No, I don't mean their Sunday best clothes. I mean, they... are... dressed up in costumes. Cap and his wife are wearing red and looking all the bit of Mr. & Mrs. Claus, while Madison makes the cutest little reindeer. "Uhm, no one told me we were dressing up. I don't have a costume."

"Oh, it's okay. I brought you one," Mad says and smiles. There is something devious in that look. She hands me a bag and shoos me away to go change.

I take the bag upstairs with me and when I open it, I'm speechless. Okay, maybe not speechless. I'm sure the whole county can hear me yelling, "Nope. Not gonna happen. No way." When I notice a giggle behind me, I spin. "I am NOT wearing this in public! It's just not going to happen. I'll pass out cookies, and I'll sing off key, but this... not gonna happen, even for you." She juts out that lower lip, gives me those big doe eyes. I shake my head no. Madison clasps her hands together, pleading, and bats those dang lashes at me. Again, I shake my head no and cross my arms in front of me. She steps closer until she's directly in front of me, then sucks her lower lip in and pushes it back out. More eyelashes blink at me. I try to shake my head no, but her hands grip my flexed arms that are still crossed. "Pretty please," she says so sweetly. "You are telling me that's the only costume you could get? Come on, Madison. It's tights! I'll never hear the end of it," I say. She whispers something into my ear. My eyes grow large, and now it's me grinning. "You promise?" I ask. Mads nods at me, emphatically. "Fine! But one snarky comment, and I'm outta there." She claps her hands together with glee, reaches up, and kisses me. Knowing I won't get much of a chance later, I deepen the kiss. My hand reaches into her hair, and her antlers get crooked, and I don't care. Only when Cap yells from downstairs, wondering what's taking so long, that I break that kiss. I motion for her to turn around, so she doesn't see me attempting to conquer this fiasco of an outfit. Let's just say my body was not made for green and white striped tights. I trip and fall three different times, trying to get the suckers on.

The fact that I caught her covering her mouth to hold back a laugh, annoys me. I've now resorted to jumping up and down while trying to yank them up. Another trip, which lands me on my bed. Using it to my advantage, I try horizontally, pulling them on, then throwing my feet up into the air. One more leap off the bed and they are on. Now for the rest of this get-up. Thank goodness, that goes smoother. I'm getting ready to put on my boots when Chloe, the reindeer, clears her throat. I gaze up to see her point to the sack again. Scared to check, I carefully take one finger and tilt it towards me and peer in. "Well, of course," I gruff. It's curled toe elf shoes. What else would it be. I growl at her. Needless to say, I stomp down the stairs. My shoes jingle the whole way.

I'll be honest, I was more like Scrooge when we got started, but the music and happy faces lightened me up. No one laughed, well, except Thomas. Paybacks will be dished out accordingly. Maybe in the form of his own elf suit and passing out gifts at the annual party.

Let's see who gets the last laugh there, buddy.

Luckily, it's one of the unseasonably warmer nights that we've had around here. Poor Santa looks a little warm with all the extra stuffing. He's definitely giving those crutches a workout. Mrs. Crosby offered her motorized scooter for the night. He almost took her up on it about halfway through the evening. The gift baskets full of tasty treats were a colossal hit. And I'll admit, so were the silly costumes.

One curious little toddler wobbled over to me and played with the shoes. He was so adorable. Little Carson let me pick him up, and he wiggled my elf ears and laughed. One of those huge baby laughs that makes you laugh, too. It made me wonder what our kids would look like, be like. Would they have dark hair or be blonde like her? Would they have my brown eyes or her blue ones? I caught her gazing at me as I danced around, swinging Carson in my arms.

It was such a good night. We even had some people join us along the way. Our party of four had grown to a cast of twelve before the night was complete. Some invited us in for hot cocoa or cider to get us warm and toasty. On one particular home, I found my fair Madison under the mistletoe. They required me to kiss her. Trust me, I had no objections. Someone snapped a photo as I held her in my arms, our lips touching. I couldn't tell you who took it because all I saw was her.

We strolled hand in hand as we ended up back where we started, the fire station. Neither of us wanted the night to end. I wanted to get out of these tights, though. Whew, they were named right. She followed me upstairs to help me get out of this contraption. Yes, it took help. I got in one more goodnight kiss before she left. Not as deep and long as I wanted, but she had her parents in the car waiting downstairs. Cap got in a pretty major workout tonight. I'm pretty sure he's beat. Even I would be after that.

CHAPTER TWELVE

MADISON

The night was amazing. I even went back over this morning to help the station wrap the gifts for the party. It's getting close. My time back in Silverdale has been a memorable one, for sure. So much so, I'm having thoughts of going back and packing my things, making it permanent. It's not a definite decision, but in this place, my folks, my friends, and Hunter are all making me reconsider my future. Dreams can change, right? My phone blows up. I've had to silence it, and it's still vibrating away. Everyone I need to talk to is here, wrapping away. I hit ignore when I glanced down. It was an unknown number. A

California unknown number. My mind wonders who it could be. Gypsy, my quirky but cool roommate, would show up. So would work. It ends up being a distraction and Sharon says, "Would you answer it already?"

I get myself up off the floor and reach into my back pocket, and pull out my phone. I walk out of the room, one hand redialing, the other, my finger in my ear. It's a bit noisy in here with all the talking, wrapping, putting together of toys. A frustrated voice on the other end answers, "What is it?"

"I'm not really sure. You're the one who keeps calling me," I reply.

"Madison. Is that you? It's about time!" the gruff man on the other end answers. Alonzo, I should have known it would be him. What on earth would he be calling me for? It's not like I was his head sous-chef or anything. I wasn't even sure I still had a job, to be perfectly honest.

"Madison, are you there?"

"Yes, Alonzo. I'm still here. What did you need?"

"I need you to come back. Gregory took a job as head chef at Chardonnay Bay. The traitor. After everything I've done for him!" I roll my eyes. Chardonnay Bay is our stiffest competition. The man would be insane not to take the job. Head chef and no more Alonzo treating him like a burger-flipper. Wait, did I hear that right? He wants me back... as sous-chef. Surely, I heard that wrong.

"Did you say you want me to come back as your sous-chef? With a raise, I'm assuming." I might as well go for it. Wait, am I even considering it? What does that mean for me and Hunter? My thoughts are swirling around in my head. What do I do?

"Yes. I need you to get on the next plane out of Whoville and get back here. NOW!" Alonzo, who sounded calm at the beginning of this rant, has now raised his voice. Exactly how I remember him being. I groan, while holding my hand over the speaker. Do I really want this? How am I going to tell Hunter and everyone I'm leaving? Am I leaving?

"It's Silverdale, Alonzo. I'll have to give it some thought. My father was in an accident, remember?" So, he's not as bad as I'd thought originally. Thank goodness. He doesn't need to know that, though.

"The offer ends at midnight. If you are not on a plane back here by then, you're fired! I've been authorized to offer you a thirty percent raise. This will be your one and only one offer. Choose wisely."

That is a pretty decent raise. I could go back, work hard, save my money and hope that no one buys the Cozy Corner before I get back. Six months is all I'd need. With what I have saved back and that money, I could make a huge down payment. Surely, everyone would understand. Hunter would get it, wouldn't he? He's waited this long. What's six more months. Right? I just need to explain it to him.

"Madison!"

"I'll let you know by midnight." Then end the call before he can say anything else. I lift my arms above me and cross them over my head, trying to clearly think this through. What do I do? Before I get all my thoughts organized, I see Hunter walk out to meet me.

"What's going on?" he asks with his hands in his back pockets. He knows something is up.

"Uhm. That was Alonzo. The head chef at Berube's. He offered me the sous-chef position. Along with a great raise."

"Are you seriously considering this? SERIOUSLY? After everything, you're going to turn around and walk away from here. From this." He motions between the two of us. He's angry and I get it. But he's not even giving me the chance to explain.

"First of all, this," I return the movement he gave me, "is new." His eyes grow large. He fists his hair and I swear I can almost see the steam coming off his body. Now, I'm getting mad.

"Yes, we aren't new. There is a history between us. Technically, we are new. You and I were kids. Now we are learning how we work as adults. I have to say, you aren't being much of an adult right now. I deserve a chance to explain."

"Are you freaking kidding me right now? You are going to walk out on me as some screwed up way of payback for me leaving you years ago? Guess what, Madison? We were kids. I had no control over where I lived. I had to go where my parents did. If this is some way of punishing me, I guess I don't know you at all."

My hand covers my stomach. I clench the pain in it. My mouth opens in a perfect O. How could he ever think I would do that? I'm not stupid. Yeah, I took the hurt and blame too far. He had no control over what happened. We had no way of knowing we'd see each other again. But to truly believe this was some kind of vendetta? "Yeah, I guess you don't know me. Do you?" I grab my coat off of the back of the chair and I slam the heavy door on my way out.

The rants are flying out of my mouth, even though no one is there to hear me. Somehow, I made it all the way back home, but don't remember one single mile. The new suitcase I had bought is thrown on the bed and I'm slinging drawer after drawer open, yelling into the silence of the room. "Hunter! You are such a jerk! I can't even believe I fell for you... again! Didn't I learn my lesson the first time?" I grab the new clothes out of the closet and throw them towards the suitcase on the bed. They don't make it. They do, however, slam into my dad, who is trying to catch items without losing his balance.

"You want to tell me what's going on, kitten? What happened? You were sitting there wrapping presents and the next thing, you storm off in your mom's car."

I run a hand through my hair. "Yeah, sorry about that. Can you give me a ride to the airport? My plane leaves in three hours." Dad hobbles over to the side of the bed and sits, resting the crutches against the wall. He pats a spot next to him. I pick a sweater up off the floor and sit next to him. Everything pours out of me. Everything. I tell him how I fell for Hunter again. How I want to buy the Cozy Corner and make it into a nice restaurant for date nights. I even tell him about how I wanted to remodel it. My desires for moving back and making a life here. I ramble on about the phone call and the job offer. Without him getting a word in, I fill him in on my idea of working for six months and save up my money. It's a reasonable idea. At least, in my head it is. He sits in silence and the one-sided conversation comes full circle when I end up crying again, telling him how Hunter is an ass, and I'm being smart to get away from him while I can.

My father wraps his arms around me and hugs me. When we pull apart, he pats me once on the knee and reaches for his crutches, pulling himself up. No advice. He just leans over and placed a kiss on top of my head and, with one good leg, exits the bedroom. My confusion is worse than ever. There's no advice, no begging me to stay. Wasn't there supposed to be pearls of wisdom laid before me? What kind of parental intervention was this, anyway? I fall backwards onto the bed, my arms spread wide. The force of my dive on the bed causes the suitcase to bounce and crash to the floor. "Well, of course!" I say with a weighted sigh.

After a few minutes, mom comes in. She pushes me over and lies on the bed with me. We both stare at the ceiling. She rolls her head to look at me and opens her mouth. It closes. I know she was about to say something about the poster. The face of my celebrity crush stares down at us from the ceiling. Finally, she rolls to her side and props herself on her elbow, so I do the same.

"I know you think your father and I are team Hunter." She strokes my hair. "We're team Madison, so we're clear." I give her a small smile. It's all I can manage. "We want you to be happy. Your dad and I remember how much you loved him. It's the hardest thing a parent can do." I give her a puzzled look, and she clarifies. "It broke my own heart to see how bad you hurt, and know that nothing I could do would patch it back up." She pulled my hand into hers. They are more aged than I remember. When did my parents get older? "We missed you. You loved him so much before. We hoped... I hoped the feelings would still be there. He came back and maybe, you would as well. It's not the same when you're not around." A lone tear streamed down mom's cheek, and I brushed it away. "Maddie, you do what makes you happy. That's all I ever want for you. If Los Angeles makes you happy, that's what you need to do. Try to visit a little more than you have been. Okay?" I nod at her and wipe away my own tears now. The ride to the airport is mostly silent. We're all too emotional to say much. I hug them both and throw my backpack over my shoulder. Mom talked me into leaving most of the new clothes there, so I'll have something to wear the next time she calls me about a family emergency. That sneaky woman.

CHAPTER

THIRTEEN

MADISON

When the plane landed and I stepped out, I was instantly hit with the warm air across my face. I had almost gotten used to the cold temps of Silverdale. Sunny skies and palm trees remind me I should probably shed this coat as soon as possible. The first Santa I see isn't covered in a bulky red suit, no he's rocking the Bermuda shorts and a beach shirt. *Toto, I'm not in Kansas anymore,* or should I say Idaho.

My first stop is to Berube's. I make it there before closing, four hours before my midnight deadline. Alonzo didn't even wait for me to put my bag down before throwing a pristine white chef's coat at me. In the back room, I pull my hair back into a tidy bun and adorn the coat. I focus at my reflection in the mirror and take a deep breath and hold it in. Alonzo yells from the kitchen for me, and I blow it out, roll my shoulders, and head for the chaos.

Berube's is busy, and the kitchen is full of the sounds of dishes clanking, steaks sizzling, eggs cracking and being whisked briskly. All the sounds and smells of a Michelin three-star restaurant, and I am a part of it. Now, a very important part of it. I dive in, taking over a station and working the dough for a delicate lobster ravioli, with hints of citrus mixed with mascarpone and saffron. This is my element and I kick butt at it. I suck in a breath when Alonzo walks to my station and dips his pinky into my filling. He takes a taste and says nothing, just nods and walks away. For him, that is the utmost praise. I peek up, seeing some of the other's looks. I've impressed the one who cannot be impressed. Pride fills me. I smile to myself and continue cooking.

My achy muscles were all worth it as I put my key into the lock and open the door. I'm greeted by Gypsy, holding a bat ready to swing. "It's me! It's me! Put the bat down."

"What are you doing here? I thought you were in Silverdale?"

"Long story. Wanna open this wine and I'll catch you up to speed?" Gypsy takes the bottle from under my arm, and heads to the kitchen. As I sit on the couch, rubbing my aching feet, I hear the pop of the cork, and sink back into the old, worn cushions. She comes over with two wine glasses and hands me one. She curls up into the other chair and tucks her feet under her. I savor that first sip before regaling her my tales of the last couple weeks. We string popcorn and nosh on more than we string as the stories unfold. She doesn't want me to move away, but thinks I'm insane for leaving "the love of my life" for a two-bit job, I hate. Not to mention a chef with a God complex. Her words, not mine. Though, I

can't really argue. I tell her my six-month plan.
She shrugs. That's her silent way of telling me
she doesn't agree with my logic, but won't fight
me on it.

The strappy little backpack purse was making
noise, my phone. I completely forgot to text my
parents. I made it home okay. When I check the
notifications of missed calls and messages, I'm
floored. Several from my parents, as expected.
The majority, however, were from Hunter. I
tossed the phone onto the couch and grabbed
another bottle of wine. With the glasses refilled,
I reached for the phone. One huge sip, and my
roommate on the edge of her seat, I go to the
voice messages first.

"There is no way you left for L.A. after how
we've been. You're still in Silverdale. Tell me
where you are so we can talk this out." Next was
one from my mom, making sure I made it home.
I shoot her a quick text. Then Hunter, "You
seriously left? Are you freaking kidding me?"
Another from mom, concerned I hadn't called.
Hunter again, "Just call me. We can talk this

through. I can't lose you again. Please, Madison." Then, one from Sharon, "Hey. Are you okay? I'm worried about you."

"Dang, you're pretty popular. And you left these people. Why again?" asks Gypsy. "I know I'm awesome and all, but seriously Maddie. I'd kill to have this many people concerned about me." When I told her I cared about her, she rolled her eyes and then gave me "the look." Sinking down further into the couch, I get ready to hear the rest of them.

Hunter yet again. "I guess I thought we were going to be a couple again. That we had a future. Why would you give up your dream job for me? I'm an idiot." Tears stream down my face. He's so heartbroken. Honestly, so am I. What am I doing? Surely, there was another way to get the money for the restaurant. I was the idiot, but it's too late now. The wine has really hit me and I'm so drowsy. Gypsy takes my phone before I can make some drunk calls and texts and I go to bed, knowing she's right.

Thank goodness I don't have to be at work until four, because my head is pounding this morning. I make my way to the medicine cabinet for some Tylenol and trudge to the kitchen when I can't find any. There has to be some in my bag. Gypsy is sitting at the kitchen table with a cup of coffee, and the headache med. I pour a cup and sit down hard in the chair. "My hair even hurts," I groan quietly. She pushes the bottle across the table and lays her head down.

"How much did we end up drinking?" she asks. Looking at the empties still on the coffee table, then back to her, "Way too many. Please tell me I didn't make any phone calls." She pulls my phone from her back pocket, and I sigh in relief. "Don't get too relaxed. Check the laptop." Looking around our small apartment, I find it still open on the counter next to the toaster. My shoulders tense, head throbs, and those creases between my eyebrows get even deeper. Ugh. Slowly, I was to the laptop like it's my executioner. Placing it between me and Gypsy, I tap the mouse pad with one eye closed, afraid to look. The screen awakens and my favorite social site is open. As I scroll, I see nothing incriminating and relief begins to set in. That is, until I realize I went live at some point in the night. Wow, were we drunk. Gypsy is in complete moral support mode in the background of my rant, pumping her fist in the air yelling, "Yeah! You tell him!" and a few other phrases that are very uncommon for my sweet friend to say.

"Delete it already! No good can come from this! Maybe no one noticed," she says. Seconds before I hit delete, I sneak a peek at the number of hearts and views. Many people saw it. She reaches over me and deletes it before I get sucked into the comment section.

"Wait!" I try to stop her. I need to know who commented what. She shuts it and pulls it away.

"But I wanted to see..."

"And while you're reading the comments, someone that maybe missed it, sees it. I'm not letting you take that chance."

"Fine! I'm going back to bed." My feet are heavy against the floor, and I collapse into the bed. I fidget around until I'm huddled in a ball, my blanket tucked all around me like a cocoon. This is my safe space.

The alarm goes off and it's time to get up and get ready for work. My headache is gone and I'm in a much better head space. I've told myself that it was probably only my local friends here saw it. It's all good. I'm standing in front of the mirror, drying my hair after my shower, when Gypsy comes in. "You had a missed call while you were in there."

I run to my dresser to get it. It has to be Hunter, and he still wants to work this out. He's going to fight for us. At least that's what I thought. It was him. However, what he said was not what I thought it was going to be. He apologized for getting mad and all the calls. The man wished me luck on all my endeavors in L.A. and that was it. It was over; we were over. I sit on the edge of the bed in shock.

"The five stages of grief," she says.

"What?" I ask her, confused.

"If you listen to the messages. They are the five stages of grief. Denial, anger, bargaining, depression, and acceptance. I must stay. He went through them faster than I would have thought, but you were only there a couple of weeks," she says.

"Nope. This is not how our stories going to end. I am not having it," I reply. I rapidly type on my phone and look for the next flight back to Silverdale. While I'm doing that, I tell her, "Well, hurry. Help me pack."

"What on Earth are you going to do?" she asks.

"I'm going to win him back. I lost him once. It is not happening again!"

"And you are going to find a flight. Today. What about work? Alonzo will fire you for sure this time. Christmas Eve is in like nine hours. You'll never get a flight out."

"Alonzo can get a new sous-chef. I'm not coming back. I'm moving back to Silverdale." Then I realize what I just said. Both of our eyes grow wide. I'm really moving back. Leaving my job doesn't bother me, but knowing I'm leaving my roommate, it sinks in. "Come with me. At least for Christmas."

"My parents will be here tomorrow, Maddie. I can't." We both realize that this is it. She hugs me tightly. Choked up, she asks, "What do I do with all your stuff. You'll have to come back." She's right. The girl is also right about the plane ticket. All flights are booked. Determined to make it home, I brainstorm aloud. Just when I'm about to give up, she gets the idea of renting a moving truck. Bingo, I can get one. While I'm calling Uber and rapidly deciding what stays and what goes, she's calling some of our friends for an emergency goodbye/moving party.

By the time I get back with the truck, the troupes have arrived and have taken down pictures and packing what few boxes they had brought with them. Our friends, who are filled in with all the holes that were left out of the live they saw, rallied. They know there is a time crunch, and if I'm going to be driving the whole way, I need to leave in the next couple of hours. When the last of the items are loaded and hugs all around, I fasten my seatbelt and am on my way. They filled the thermos with hot coffee instead of cocoa. I'll need the caffeine fix if I'm going to be driving all night and part of the day.

CHAPTER

FOURTEEN

MADISON

The quaint sign in Silverdale is finally in view, and it's a ghost town. I expected that. Everyone is at the Christmas Party held at Pavilion. The clock on my phone tells me, if I hurry, I can run to mom and dad's and get cleaned up. Like a madwoman, I drive home, running through a stop sign. Of course, no one is in sight until the flashing lights come on. "Are you kidding me right now?" I say to the heavens. The officer strolls up to the window, pad in hand. I roll it down and see that it's Thomas, Sharon's husband.

"Madison? Is that really you?" he asks. "My best friend is pretty tore up because of you."

"I plan on making it right. You're not at the party?"

"Just making my rounds and heading over there," he answers. I give the man my sweetest smile. "What?"

"What's the chance I could get a police escort to the party? Let me go change and fix my hair, twenty minutes tops." I bat my eyelashes for effect.

"Fine. Only because you are my best friend's girl. That and Sharon would kill me if I didn't. You are here for Hunter, right?" I cross my heart. He shakes his head and heads back to his rig. I follow him back to my parents where he calls over the loudspeaker, "Twenty minutes." I nod and jump out of the moving truck and dash for the house. At exactly twenty minutes, he pulls back up outside, and I exit the house. He gives

me a whistle and holds open the door to the back
seat.

"Are you serious?" I ask.

"I'm just making sure you don't flee the scene
this time. Hunter loves you, you know that,
right?" I nod and get in.

"I love him, too. He'll find out how much
tonight."

We walk in to the Pavilion together and Sharon
leans in giving him a kiss, then notices me.

"Maddie! You're back!" She throws her arms
around me and we hug.

I look around, trying to spot Hunter. He is
nowhere to be found. My mother sees me though
and rushes over. We walk arm and arm towards
Santa and all the action. A massive tree is lit up
and full of brightly colored ornaments. Piles and
piles of presents surround it. Santa sits in an
ornate chair and mom begs me to get a picture
with him. I protest, wanting to find the man I
came for. Mom's not having it. Not seeing my
dad, I can only assume she talked him into
playing the part. In the line I stand, waiting to

talk to my dad. My eyes constantly scanning the room. Hunter still isn't in sight. Maybe he's not even here.

Once I get to the front of the line, I awkwardly sit on my dad's lap. He says nothing and just listens as I spill my guts. "I really screwed things up this time. Being a fancy chef is what I thought I wanted. Turns out, what I want it right here in Silverdale. I love Hunter. He loves me, too. Or at least he did. I want to buy the Cozy Corner and make it a place of my own. Where people will go on dates. A place where lovers will go for an enjoyable meal. The place where someone proposes over dessert." I ramble on and on before it comes around to Hunter again. "Santa, I haven't been the best person. Can I still make a Christmas wish?" He nods. "Can you make it not too late for me and him? While you at it, can you throw in a restaurant?" He gives me a jovial laugh and HO, HO, HO. I kiss him on the cheek and go back to standing by my mom. The kids now surround, anxiously waiting for gifts to be passed out.

Out, from behind a sleigh, come several elves. I laugh with joy and wipe away a stray tear when I see one is my Hunter. He hasn't noticed me, being busy passing out gifts to all the children. Radiant faces and laughter fill the room as child after child rips away the wrapping paper to find their surprises.

Santa gets Hunter's attention. He points in my direction. That's when he stops in his tracks. Our eyes are locked on each other. He heads towards me, but Santa stops him and whispers something. They turn their backs to us and walk to the sleigh. From behind me, I hear my dad's voice. I whip around in confusion. "Dad! Wait. You're not Santa? Then who was I spilling my guts to?" Spinning back around, I'm face to face with Hunter and Santa. "If you aren't dad..." he gives me a wink and nudges the man of my dreams, who hands me a box. Slowly, I peer at Santa and then at the box. I open it to find a key. Now, I'm even more confused.

Santa lowers his beard, and it's Stan, the owner of Cozy Corner. Val, his wife, comes up and wraps her arm around his waist. They beam at me. "One of Santa's helpers told us how bad you wanted the restaurant. We would love for you to own it and make it into the eatery of your dreams. Silverdale could use some place fancy," Val states.

"We'll work out the down payment and you can do contract for deed. I'll get the papers drawn up, and we'll sign everything next week, if that works for you."

"Are you kidding? Yes! Of course, yes! You're sure?" I ask.

"Madison, you grew up loving that place. We don't have kids of our own. Watching you hang out there, grow up there. It was like watching our girl grow up," Val sniffled. "Now, you two go enjoy yourselves. For heaven's sake, kiss and make up, already."

I gave Stan and Val the biggest hugs, before turning to mom and dad. Keys in hand, I shook them and squealed with excitement. Last, but not least, I turned to Hunter. "Didn't think I'd see you in that get-up again."

"Yeah, well. The kids like it," he said shyly.

"I've still got a few things to do here. Can I catch up with you in about thirty minutes and give you a ride home? We need to talk."

"No."

"No? Uhm, okay?" He says and scratches his fingers through his hair, perplexed.

"I mean, yeah. You can give me a ride home. No, I need to do something before you run off." It's then that I take his face between my palms and plant the biggest kiss on him. Some of the children glance up from their gifts to announce, "Ew." While a few of the adults gaze over and say, "Aww." We break apart, both of us with pink cheeks of embarrassment.

He steps backwards, walking away, motioning behind him that he has to go. Hunter ends up stumbling over a large candy cane that had fallen over. He grabs it and catches his balance. Nice save. I wave at him, chuckling. The elf of my dreams disappears through some doors marked "Santa's Workshop."

It's about fifty minutes before he emerges. Now dressed in well-worn faded jeans and a navy-blue Henley. There is something so sexy about a guy pushing his sleeves up, flexing those muscles as he does. Holes in jeans that you just know came from hard work. Did I mention the work boots? Swoon worthy. I guess I was so busy keeping my guard up; I didn't realize just how handsome this man truly was now. That crooked grin, those eyes. A girl could get used to seeing that every day.

CHAPTER FIFTEEN

HUNTER

There is something new in the way her eyes gaze at mine. A warmth or, dare I say, longing in them. Each step closer, it becomes clearer. This is the look I've been waiting for. There is forever in her eyes now, and it takes my breath away. I place my palm on the small of her back and kiss her cheek. "Sorry, that took so long. Are you ready to go?" She nods yes, and I help her on with her coat. "You look beautiful tonight, Mad. I'm so glad you're back." Needing to ask her if it's for good. I remember the key that Stan and Val gave her. I open the door for her, and she slides in. On the way to my side, I turn my eyes to the heaven's and mouth a silent "Thank you, Santa."

We sit in silence for several minutes. She finally turns to me and tells me, "I'm sorry. I was taking the move out on you. The fact I had never moved on, out on you. Everything in general, I took out on you, and it wasn't fair." I glance over at her and smile softly.

"Well, at least you admit it," I say with a laugh. I catch her scrunching her face and add, "too soon?" I tap the brake and the car slides on the ice. Her hand grasps my thigh and I instinctively throw my arm out in front of her to protect her. My truck slides off the side of the road. There is a tiny ditch, but it's enough that we are stuck. I hop out and she slides over and takes the wheel. I try to push it while she tries to drive out. The truck slides more off the road.

I grab my phone and call one of the local guys for a tow, but he's out on another call. It's going to be awhile. We decide to make the best of it, and I ask her about her taking over the diner. Even in the dark, the only light coming from the dash, her eyes light up. She has so many ideas, great ones. I love seeing her like this. Madison slips and says "we" while talking about the new place.

I stop her and ask who "we" are. She gets shy and tucks her hair behind her ear. "You and me. If you still want me in your life after all the trouble, I've caused you." Now's the time. I reach for the thermos behind the seat and pull it out.

"You're kidding right? You have a thermos?" she asks.

"Never leave home without it," I say and hand it to her. As she unscrews the cap, something clanks. She looks up at me, puzzled. Madison takes the top completely off and inside the lid is a diamond ring. Her eyes well with tears as she pours it into her hand. I pick up the ring and slide it onto her finger. "Madison, I have loved you for so long. Life went sideways, but we are together again. It's destiny. I'm never going to leave you again, and I hope you feel the same." She nods, speechless. "There is nothing in this world that's ever going to keep us apart again, I promise you that. Will you marry me?"

Madison throws her arms around me and tells me yes. Relief floods me. She pulls back and looks into my eyes. "How long have you been planning on asking me?"

"The hot cocoa is fresh from the party, I swear." She gives me a little shove and asks about the proposal. "Truthfully?"

"Yeah, the truth. How long have you had this ring?" she asks.

"I brought it with me when I moved back to Silverdale. I bought it on the way back into town. Granted, back then it was in a jewelry box."

"You've been carrying it around all this time?"

"Well, no. It sat in the box on my nightstand. Until the day I saw you at the fire station. That day, I got the ring and put it in my pocket. I've been carrying it ever since." Her hand lays across her heart now. She scoots closer to me, and we snuggle up. I tilt her chin up and I bring her lips to mine for a kiss. Things are getting a little warm in the truck's cab. Exactly like what happens every time we are alone, someone interrupts us. This time, the bright lights of the tow truck are beaming in at us.

Darrell, the driver of the truck, comes up beside us. I roll down the steamed-up window and the man props his arm in the window and leans in. Madison's cheeks are blazing with embarrassment. "Don't worry folks. I'll have you back on the road in a jiffy." He slaps his hand on the sill and leaves, getting to work. A few minutes later, we are pulled back onto the road. I step out of the vehicle and reach in my wallet to pay the man.

"Put that away, Hunter. Heck, you weren't even really stuck." Shoot, the window is still down. Man, I hope she didn't hear that. I cough loudly and quickly urge the man back to his tow truck. He heads off to his next call and I make my way back to my own truck.

"Hunter Dean! Did you really just pretend to be stuck so you could propose to me and I couldn't run?"

"It worked, didn't it?" I give her my most wicked smile.

"And who all was in on this minor detour you had planned?"

"Who do you think gave me the hot cocoa?" She rolls her eyes and shakes her head at me.

"I think it's time for a little payback... and you are going to help me," she says devilishly.

Back at the Hoover's
Madison

I walk into the door and my parent's jump from their seats to greet me. They are expecting a wedding announcement. I can see it on their faces. "Where's Hunter? We thought maybe you guys had a talk."

"Oh, we had a talk alright."

"He didn't ask you anything important?" mom questions.

"He did." I pause for effect and it's working. Mom is wringing her hands and dad gets a panicked expression. "I told him no."

"What do you mean, honey? You told him no about what?" dad asks.

"He proposed, and I told him no. It's too soon. Not to mention, I'm going to be so busy with the new restaurant. He's busy at the fire station. Especially with you gone, dad. It's not good timing." I can hardly keep a straight face.

"Uhm. So, what happened after you told him you would not marry him?" mom asks.

"That arrogant man! We got into this huge fight. He had already started planning the wedding! He was yelling. How could I ever be with someone so temperamental and emotional? I mean, seriously." I gave this huge dramatic sigh and plopped on the couch. My feet now propped on the coffee table for full effect as I prop my arms behind my head. "Man, dodged a bullet there." Mom and dad sit down on each side of me, each taking one of my hands. Dad has actual beads of sweat on his forehead. This is going to be priceless. "I am so sorry, Madison. We never should have gotten so involved. We wanted you to come home and be happy."

I raise off the couch, take their hands and put them in each other's. Now standing directly in front of them, I take a bow. They glance at each other and then at me. Hunter comes into the room with the thermos. I finger gun shoot my victory, "Gotcha!"

My fiancé puts his arm around my waist and kissed me on the cheek. With the other, carrying the thermos, he hands it back to mom. "Here's your thermos, Mrs. Hoover. It worked like a charm." He winks at mom. The two of us bust out laughing. Between the hysterics, he adds, "Sorry. She made me do it."

They don't know whether to hug me or strangle me. They do both. Dad pops the bottle of champagne they had ready for us and we celebrate. Hunter decides he doesn't know or care what time it is where his parents are. He calls them and we all video chat, telling them the news. Funny thing is, they somehow knew we were going to call and had their own champagne flutes ready. I give my parents a side eye and they do a really lousy job of looking innocent.

There's never a dull moment with this family.

Epilogue: New Year's Eve

Madison

It's almost midnight, and Hunter and I are sitting in the empty restaurant. The one that we now own, together, having signed the papers today. We are sitting on top of the main counter facing each other. Just like an all too familiar eighties classic. What can I say? I've really always wanted to do this. Instead of the classic birthday cake and candles between us, me in a bridesmaid dress and him in a sweater vest, it's slightly different.

I am dressed in white. My wedding dress, to be exact. My handsome groom is wearing a tux. Sitting between us is an enormous slab of wedding cake, no candles, and a brand new, glitzed out thermos we got as a wedding gift. Hey, it's our thing. We are waiting anxiously for my alarm to go off. At the stroke of midnight, it does. Yeah, yeah, the ringtone may be the song from the ending of my favorite movie. He's going along with it. Why, you ask? Because he loves me, of course!

He leans over and gives me a lingering New Year's kiss. When he pulls back, he asks, "So what happens next, Mrs. Dean?"

"A thermos always full of hot cocoa, and a life full of shenanigans, Mr. Dean."

"And they lived happily ever after"